卖—小—金鱼儿嘞……

图书在版编目（CIP）数据

小金鱼儿 / 保冬妮著；黄捷绘 .—乌鲁木齐：新疆青少年出版社，
2010.3

（"小时候"中国图画书系列）

ISBN 978-7-5371-8145-7

I . 小… II . ①保…②黄… III . 图画故事—中国—当代

IV .I287.8

中国版本图书馆 CIP 数据核字（2010）第 040009 号

"小时候"中国图画书系列

小 金 鱼 儿

保冬妮 / 文　黄捷 / 绘

策　　划：北京花婆婆文化创意有限责任公司

责任编辑：许国萍　刘悦铭

美术编辑：查　璇

装帧设计：隋燕冬

出 版 人：徐　江

出版发行：新疆青少年出版社　（乌鲁木齐市北京北路 29 号　830012）

经　　销：新华书店

印　　制：北京尚唐印刷包装有限公司

开　　本：16 开

印　　张：3

字　　数：3 千字

版　　次：2010 年 5 月第 1 版

印　　次：2015 年 11 月第 5 次印刷

印　　数：22001—27000 册

书　　号：ISBN 978-7-5371-8145-7

定　　价：15.00 元

「小时候」中国图画书系列

小金鱼儿

The Little Goldfish

保冬妮／文　黄　捷／绘

北京记忆

新疆青少年出版社

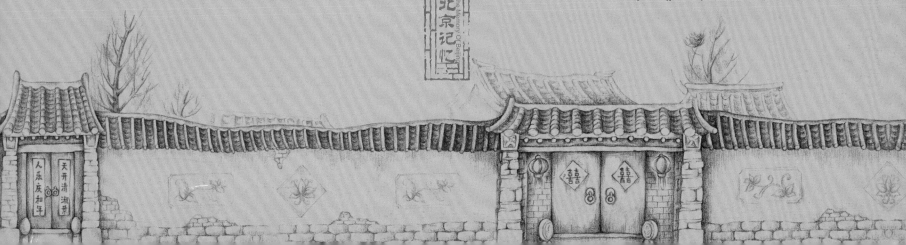

林大爷是我们院卖金鱼儿的，我特喜欢他。

"爷爷，那一脑袋疙瘩的叫什么呀？"

"傻孩子，那叫绣球。"

小喜子爱跟着卖金鱼儿的老林头**屁颠儿屁颠儿**地追，
因为呀，小喜子他妈不给他买小金鱼儿。

"头一天买了，二一天就死了。你那是折腾小金鱼儿还是喜欢小金鱼儿呀？让它们在你林大爷那儿好好活着，有多好。"

听听，多唠叨！

"我要小金鱼儿……" 就这话，小喜子 嘟嘟嚷嚷

能跟妈妈 嚷 一天，磨得全院子的人耳朵都起糨子了。

"**得了**，喜子，在大爷这儿看看就行了。"

"留点神儿啊，缸可深……" 林大爷说完，往车上的鱼缸里舀上一盆小金鱼儿，又上街去了。

"小金鱼儿，你从**哪儿**来的呀？"
小喜子往上一**蹿**，
一伸手，**哎哟**，
拽着小金鱼儿啦……

小喜子骑上了鱼！

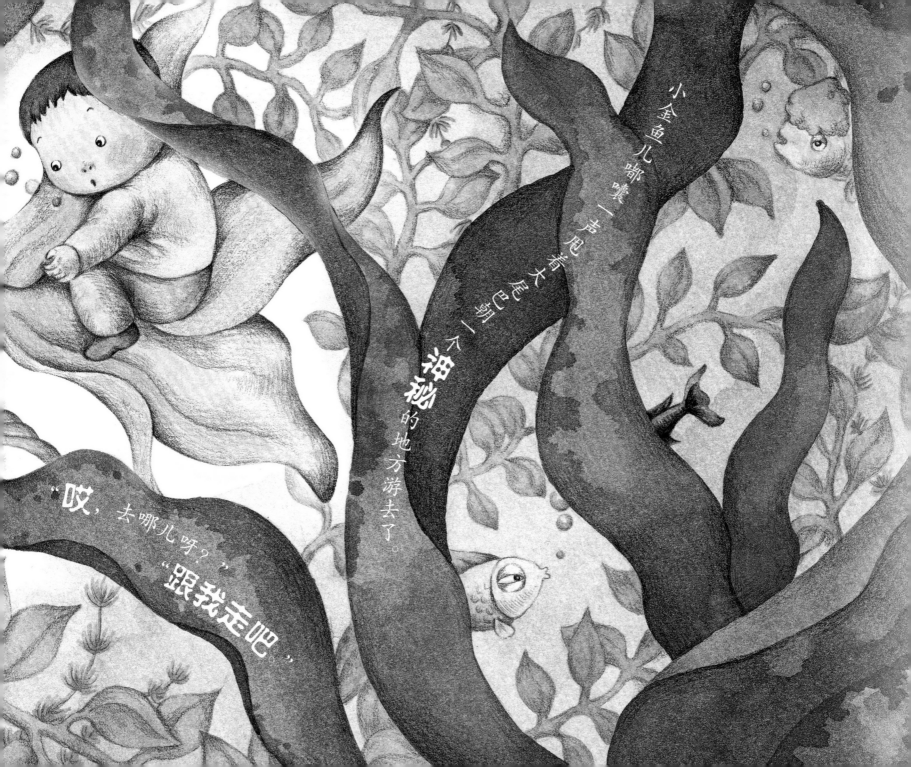

小金鱼儿嘟囔一声甩着大尾巴朝一个神秘的地方游去了。

"哎，去哪儿呀？"

"跟我走吧。"

"走着！"

小金鱼儿一甩尾巴，背着小喜子就**进去了**。

"绣球奶奶……"

小金鱼儿叫着，游
到了鱼精奶奶的身边。

"杀死他了？"

"还没呢。"

"小喜子喜欢咱，他想知道咱们金鱼儿是怎么来的。"

小喜子凑到鱼精奶奶的身边："您是**鱼精奶奶**？
哎呀，林爷爷也得叫您奶奶吧？"

"林爷爷 **是谁**?"

"就是 **卖小金鱼儿的** 林爷爷呗。"

"他只是卖小金鱼儿的，岁数不过半百。我呀，已经活了从鲫鱼变金鱼、从池养到盆养的**七百年**呢，经历过宋、元、明、清四个朝代，你们人哪，都是**我的小孙孙**！"

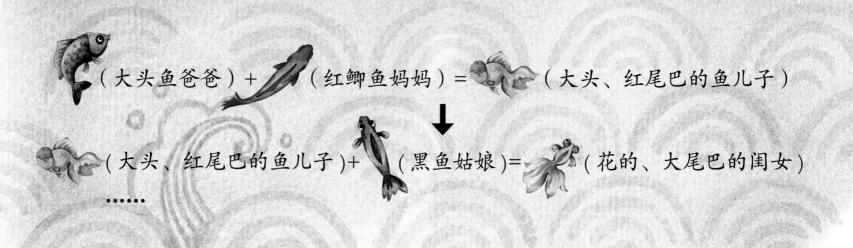

（大头鱼爸爸）+ （红鲫鱼妈妈）= （大头、红尾巴的鱼儿子）

（大头、红尾巴的鱼儿子）+ （黑鱼姑娘）= （花的、大尾巴的闺女）

……

小喜子惊讶地问："那您也是**鲫鱼变的吗？**"

鱼精奶奶头顶大红帽，一甩尾巴："没有哪条金鱼是**一眨么眼儿**就从鲫鱼变金鱼的，那是一代一代慢慢儿变的。"

"哦，我知道。就跟我们同学海伦一样，她妈妈是中国人，她爸爸是美国人，她就是有**黑头发、绿眼睛**的女孩儿。"

不等小喜子说完，鱼精奶奶早**没影儿了**。

小喜子**一个猛子钻**出头来，说：

"哎哟！鱼精奶奶呢？……"

"**你听**！谁喊你了？"小金鱼儿一甩尾巴，
赶紧走了。

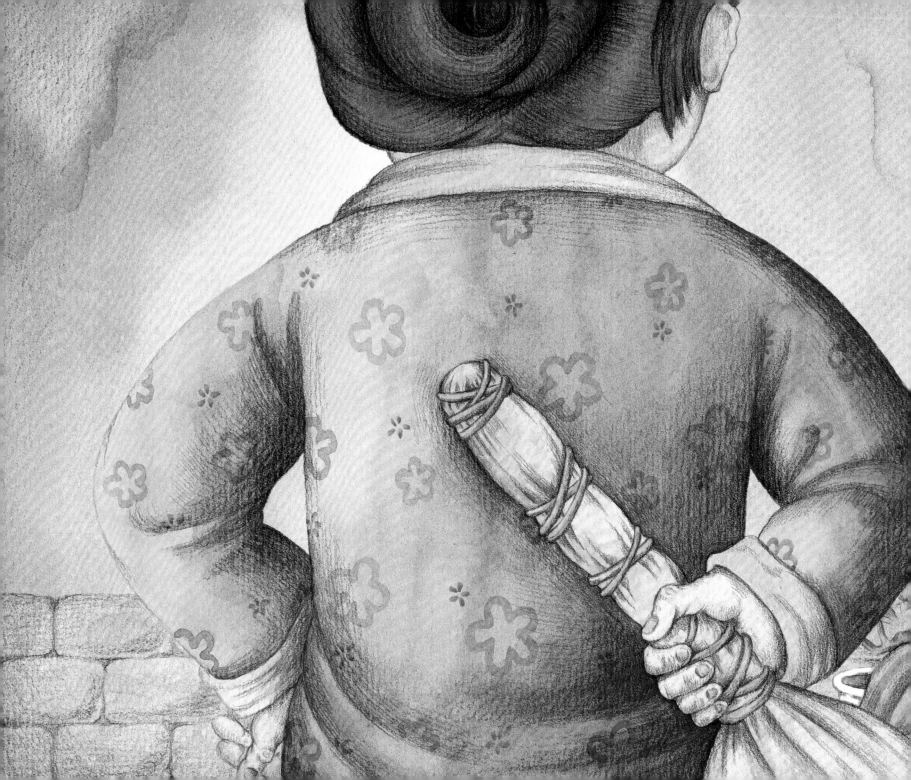

"喜子，你怎么玩到缸里去了？看我不**打**你！"

"人家又不是故意的，**我改**，还不成……"

小金鱼儿
The Little Goldfish

■ 游走了的老时光

喜欢小金鱼儿的人，一定也会喜欢北京的胡同儿。因为，"卖小金鱼儿嘞——"的叫卖声和胡同是连在一起的。如果你过去曾经在北京的胡同里住过，就一定听到过那夏天午后从窗户外钻进来的悠长的叫卖声："卖小金鱼儿嘞——"特别好听。那叫唤声让孩子们心里都像被猫抓了似的往胡同里跑。那时候街上干净，也清净，没那么多车，挺安全。小孩儿们围着卖金鱼儿的老头儿看啊看啊……常常忘了回家。

这是过去北京小朋友最普遍的游戏生活；而现在，孩子们都在电脑和游戏机营造的虚拟世界里游弋了，还有谁在意小金鱼儿这种游动缓慢又悄无声息的慢生活宠物呢？事实上，恰恰是这缓慢的生活节奏，成就了金鱼儿的美丽，也恰恰是那近千年点点滴滴的进化，造就了小金鱼儿如今异彩纷呈的品种和高雅娴静的仪态。

快与慢，像是时光透过生命之树所呈现的那样，明亮和阴翳，谁也离不开谁，谁也代替不了谁。在快生活几乎已经把我们的休闲时光吞噬一空的时候，试着静静地与小金鱼儿一起放慢呼吸，在清澈而舒缓的感觉里，你会忽然找回一种久违了的放松。

保冬妮：中国作家协会会员、儿童文学作家、心理咨询师。

我喜欢小金鱼儿，也喜欢北京的胡同儿。小时候住景山公园东边的三眼井胡同，夏天，老有悠长的叫卖声从窗户外钻进来："卖小金鱼儿嘞——"特别好听，叫唤声让孩子们心里都像被猫抓了似的往胡同里跑。那时候街上干净，也清净，没那么多车，挺安全。小孩儿们围着卖金鱼儿的老头儿看啊看啊……常常忘了回家。

作者已在海内外出版作品六十余部、三百万余字，著作曾荣获"第四届全国优秀儿童文学奖"、"第五届国家优秀少儿图书奖"、"冰心儿童图书奖"、"冰心儿童文学新作奖"、"新闻出版总署向青少年推荐的百种优秀图书"等荣誉，现为全国妇联《超级宝宝》杂志主编。

黄捷：80后，画家。

毕业于清华大学美术学院。

2008年开始从事图画书创作，其作品注重对细节的描绘，散发出一种精致而温和的魅力。

主要作品：《小金鱼儿》《水牛儿》和《小布老虎》系列。

平时喜欢旅行、音乐、电影和不听话的小朋友。

雪芹（Qin Xue Herzberg）：翻译

出生于北京，毕业于北京师范大学中文系。1987年赴美国加尔文大学留学，自1990年在加尔文大学执教高年级汉语至今。雪芹在中美两地的报刊、杂志上已发表了上百篇文章。她和丈夫Larry喜欢到世界各地旅行。雪芹热爱动物，最喜欢的小动物是猫。

何乐礼（Larry Herzberg）：翻译

美国加尔文大学汉语和日语教授。他热爱属于中国的一切事物。2008年，他和妻子雪芹合作出版了一本有关中国旅游的书，受到了广大读者的赞誉。何乐礼多才多艺，喜爱写作和旅行，还是位出色的小提琴手，每年都会在美国的大溪流城交响乐团演奏130场。

小金鱼儿 The Little Goldfish

I Story / Bao Dongni
I Drawing / Huang Jie
I Translation / Qin Xue Herzberg & Larry Herzberg

英文翻译

"Selling little goldfish! …"

Grandpa Lin is from our courtyard. He sells goldfish. I like him very much.
"Grandpa Lin, what about the one with all the lumps on its head, what is he called?"
"Child, that one is called the silk ball."

Little Merry loves to follow the old man Lin to see the goldfish because Little Merry's mother wouldn't buy the goldfish for him. "You buy it on the first day, only to have it die on you by the second day! Do you really like the goldfish or do you want to torture the little thing? Let him stay happily with Grandpa Lin. That's a much better idea." Mother said.
Listen to her, nagging on and on endlessly.

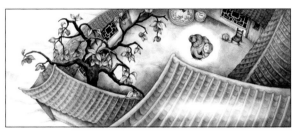

"I want the litter goldfish! I want the little goldfish! ..." Little Merry mumbled to his mother ceaselessly until the neighbors from the same courtyard felt their ears go numb.

"That's enough, Little Merry. Just come over here and watch it. Be careful. The water vat is very deep..." After saying that, Grandpa Lin transferred some goldfish from the water vat to his cart, then left for his rounds.

"Little goldfish, where do you come from?" Little Merry said to the goldfish. He leapt up and extended his hand into the water vat. Ah! He got hold of the goldfish's tail...

Thump. Little Merry found himself riding on the little goldfish.
"Hey, where are we going?"
"Follow me." the little goldfish muttered, then swung his big tail around and swam off toward a mysterious place.

"Strange, how come there is a huge palace off in the distance?"

"Let's go in." The little goldfish swung his big tail and took Little Merry in.

"Ah, it is Grandmother, the Silk Ball." the little goldfish cried out and swam toward the fish spirit.

"Hey! How can you bring back a child?" The old fish spirit asked vigilantly.
"This little boy likes me. He wants to know where goldfish come from."
said the little goldfish.

"Did you tell him?"
"Not yet."
Little Merry went next to her and asked: "Are you the fish spirit? Wow! Even Grandpa Lin probably has to call you Grandmother?"
"Who is Grandpa Lin?"
"The old man who sells goldfish."

"He sells little goldfish and he is only under fifty. I, on the other hand, have gone through the transformation from a carp to a goldfish, from being in a pond to being in a fish tank over a period of more than seven hundred years! I have gone through the four dynasties of Song, Yuan, Ming and Qing! Even you humans are all my great-grandchildren!"

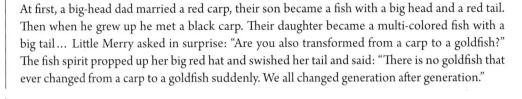

At first, a big-head dad married a red carp, their son became a fish with a big head and a red tail. Then when he grew up he met a black carp. Their daughter became a multi-colored fish with a big tail… Little Merry asked in surprise: "Are you also transformed from a carp to a goldfish?" The fish spirit propped up her big red hat and swished her tail and said: "There is no goldfish that ever changed from a carp to a goldfish suddenly. We all changed generation after generation."

"Oh, I know. It's like my classmate, Helen. Her mom is Chinese and her dad is American, so she has green eyes and black hair." Little Merry was still talking, but the fish spirit had already gone.

Little Merry dove and stuck his head out of the water. "Hey, where is the fish spirit?"
"Listen, someone's calling you." The little goldfish swung its tail around and left in a hurry.

"Little Merry! How could you get into the water vat to play? Wait and see how I'm going to punish you!"
"I didn't do it on purpose. I'll be better in the future. OK?"

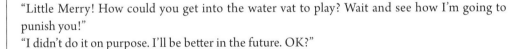

"Selling little goldfish!"

新一代鱼儿嘞……